First published in 2012 in Great Britain by
Barrington Stoke Ltd
18 Walker Street, Edinburgh, EH3 7LP

www.barringtonstoke.co.uk

ISBN: 978-1-84299-907-3

Printed in China by Leo

Contents

Chapter 1
Green Slime

Tony rode his motorbike up the dark alley and parked outside his dad's magic shop. It was late, but the lights were still on inside.

The magic shop had to stay open late. Some of the people who came to buy stuff there had to keep out of the sun. That was because Tony's dad's shop wasn't the kind of magic shop that sold jokes and toys. It sold the real thing, to people who needed it.

As Tony walked in to the shop, he nearly knocked over a man who was looking in the glass case by the door.

"Sorry!" Tony said. "I didn't see you there!"

The man didn't say anything, but he turned and glared at Tony. At least, Tony thought he was glaring. It was a bit hard to tell because he had on a big hat and dark glasses, and he had a thick grey beard which covered almost his whole face.

In most places, the man would have looked a bit odd. But you got all kinds of people in magic shops.

Tony smiled. "Do you need any help?" he asked. "I'm Tony Kim, the owner's son. Sorry the shop's a bit of a mess. It can be hard for me to find things sometimes, and I've worked here for years!"

The man didn't say anything. He just turned back and stared at the case again.

"All right, er ... good," Tony said at last. "I'll leave you to it, then."

He walked over to the till, where Jazz was sitting. Jazz was an art student who worked as the shop assistant. She had blue hair and lots of tattoos. Tony leaned over to whisper to her.

"How long has that bloke been in here?"

"Ages!" Jazz hissed. "He's freaking me out. Can you get rid of him?"

They both looked at the guy in the coat. He didn't look like he was going to leave any time soon.

"How can I get rid of him?" Tony whispered. "We don't close for hours."

"It's your shop," said Jazz. "Kick him out!"

"It's not my shop," Tony said. "It's my dad's."

"But your dad's in France!" Jazz said. "He won't be back till Friday. That bloke can't stay here till Friday!"

"Oh, come on. He's got to leave some time," Tony said. "I'm going to go and check on that potion in the back room."

"Wimp," Jazz said in a hiss.

Tony just shrugged, and went into the back room.

The back room was Tony's dad's office. Most of the time it was even more of a mess than the rest of the shop. But Tony had cleared the junk off the desk that morning. He'd been trying to make a potion.

It was meant to be a speed potion, to make the person who drank it move faster. But it had all gone a bit wrong.

First Tony had run out of horse-hair. His dad's notes said that rabbit fur would work just as well. But they hadn't said how much rabbit fur to use, so Tony had put in a lot. Rabbits were slower than horses, right?

But now Tony wondered if he'd used too much. The potion was meant to end up white but his one had gone pink. He'd left it on the desk when he went out, in the hope it would change colour.

Well, he was half in luck. The potion wasn't pink any more.

Now it was dark green.

How on Earth had it ended up green?

"Jazz, did you touch my potion?" Tony yelled.

"I haven't been near it," Jazz called back.

“Then why is it green?” Tony picked the jar up and gave it a shake.

“Because you’re crap at magic?”

“Hey, I’m still learning!” Tony protested. He stared at the jar. “And even I’m not this bad.” Now the green stuff had started to bubble and smoke. There was no way it should be getting – hot! Tony yelped and let go of the jar.

The jar hit the stone floor and smashed into a thousand pieces. Green slime splashed all over the room.

“What have you done, Tony?” Jazz shouted from the front room.

“It wasn’t me, it was the jar!” he shouted back. “I couldn’t keep hold of it!”

The pool of slime was spreading fast. Tony took a step back.

“Oh, so it just jumped out of your hand, did it?” Jazz called. For all he couldn’t see her, Tony could tell she was rolling her eyes.

“I think it might have done.” Tony looked at the pool of slime. It was moving as if it was alive. It was growing, too. There was far more slime now than there had been in the jar. It had started to swell up into a big blob.

"Jazz, I could use some help in here," Tony yelled. "I think I'm going to need a mop."

Then the blob started to move towards him. Tony took a few more steps back.

"Or maybe a gun."

Chapter 2
Stolen Goods

By now the blob of slime was as a big as a small dog and it had taken on the shape of a giant slug. It had no eyes or ears, but it seemed to know Tony was there. It was heading for his feet.

As the blob oozed towards Tony, it left a trail of wet slime behind it on the floor. It moved over a book, and the pages went black and started to curl. Tony gulped. If it could rot paper that fast, what would it do to human skin?

He climbed on top of the desk as fast as he could.

That was when Jazz opened the door. "Tony, what are you doing – ?" she began. Then she saw the blob and jumped back. "What on Earth is that thing?"

"I don't know, but don't let it get out!" Tony said. "That slime could destroy all the stuff in the shop – or worse!" Tony didn't want to find out what would happen if the slime got a chance to mix with more magic.

"What is it?" Jazz asked. "Is it your potion?"

"Well, it's not my dinner!" said Tony. "Help me get rid of it, Jazz!"

Now slime had started to crawl up the side of the desk. The wood turned black as it crawled over it and Tony could smell the rot it left behind. He backed up till he hit the wall.

"How do we kill it?" Jazz asked.

"How do I know?" Tony snapped. "It's not like I've ever made a slime monster before!" He looked around for ideas. Salt! Salt could be used to end most spells, and it was bad for slugs, right? “Um … throw some salt at it!” he said.

“I’ll go and get some.” Jazz ran out of the office and into the front shop.

That left Tony stuck on top of the desk. As he watched, the slime rose up over the edge.

It was going to reach him before Jazz got back. He had to find a way to slow it down!

Tony looked at the shelf above the desk. There was all kinds of junk up there. Could any of it help?

Books? No.

Candles? No.

A tin of cat food? No. What was that even doing up there?

Wait – there was a bag of herbs! Tony didn’t know what the herbs were, but they had to be magic. He grabbed the bag and threw it at the slime.

“Eat that, slime monster!” he yelled.

It did. The bag sank into the slime with a noise that sounded a lot like a burp. The slime went still for a moment, then it started to shake. Then it grew to twice its size.

"Oh, crap," said Tony, as it started moving towards him again.

"I've got the salt!" Jazz ran in with a big pot. "What do I do?"

"Just throw it at it!" Tony said. He was pressed right up into the corner now. The slime had nearly reached his feet.

Jazz threw the pot of salt at the slime. The pot hit its target, and sank in with a wet slurp. The slime began to wobble.

"I meant you to throw the salt, not the whole pot!" Tony shouted.

"Well, that's not what you said!" Jazz shouted back. They both stared at the blob. It was still wobbling.

Wobbling quite hard, in fact. As if it was going to –

"Look out!" Tony yelled.

That was when the blob exploded.

Green slime flew all over the room. Tony threw his arms up in front of his face just in time. Some slime hit his left hand. It stung like mad and he wiped it off as fast as he could.

Jazz had ducked, but some slime had landed in her hair. She wiped it off with her sleeve and pulled a face. "You guys should be paying me a lot more than you are."

Tony got down from the desk. The office looked like a bomb had gone off in it, if bombs were made of slime. There was green stuff all over the walls and smashed glass all over the floor. Half of the desk was black with rot.

Tony tapped the side of the desk with his foot. The wood was so weak that his toe left a dent in it. He let out a groan. "I think my dad's going to need a new desk."

"I think your dad's going to need a new office," Jazz said. She shook her head. "Tony, this is going to take hours to clean up and I can't stay late tonight."

Tony didn't want to stay late any more than Jazz did. He gave her a tired smile. "Let's just leave it till the morning," he said. "It's not like it's going to get worse between now and then, right?"

He hoped it wouldn't. You could never be too sure with magic.

They walked out into the front shop. "At least none of the slime got out here," Tony said. "And hey, I think we scared off that creepy guy! That's one bit of good news."

"Um, Tony?" Jazz said. She pointed at a glass case on the other side of the room. "It looks like he's not the only thing that's gone."

The case had been smashed open, and it was empty.

The shop had been robbed.

Tony put his head in his hands. "Oh, crap."

Chapter 3
Magic Mirror

As far as Tony could tell, nothing was missing from the rest of the shop. Only the glass case had been smashed.

That made him feel worse, not better. The thief hadn't just grabbed what he could. He'd wanted what was in that case.

"Should we call the police?" Jazz asked.

"There's no point," Tony told her. "The police are no help when it comes to magic. They would think all the stuff in the shop is fake. They wouldn't try very hard to get it back."

Even if the police did try, what could Tony tell them? He hadn't got a good look at the thief. The hat and dark glasses had hidden the man's face. He didn't even know what had been stolen!

There was only one thing Tony could do now.

He pulled a face.

"I'm going to have to call my dad."

Tony's dad often went off on trips round the world. He went looking for new kinds of magic he could sell.

In the past, he'd had to close the shop while he was gone. But since Tony had turned 17, his dad had been able to leave him in charge.

A few things had gone wrong. But this was the worst by far.

Tony rang his dad's number. He half hoped his dad wouldn't pick up the phone, but he was out of luck.

"Ah, Tony!" his dad said. "I've been meaning to call you. I ran into my old friend Boris! I haven't seen him in years. How are things at the shop?"

Tony's dad sounded like he was in a good mood, which made Tony feel worse. If Tony told him about the robbery, he'd come right home. It would spoil his trip. And it might be a long time before he saw Boris again.

But maybe Tony was just making excuses. Maybe he just didn't want to have to tell his dad the bad news.

The lie came out before he had time to think it through.

"Er, things are fine," he said. "We're OK. I just wanted to ask, um ... that glass case by the door. The one with the metal stand. What's in it?"

"Next to the door?" His dad stopped to think. "That's ... well, it should be an ivory curse box. It's got the ashes of a deadly snake inside. You can call the snake up and give it orders. Why do you want to know? It's not missing, is it?" He sounded worried.

Tony's heart was beating fast. "No!" he lied. "No, it's not. I just, um ... this guy was looking at it. I didn't want to sell it when I didn't know what it was."

"Well, that was a smart move," his dad said. "That thing could do a lot of harm in the wrong hands. If he comes in again, tell him he'll have to wait till I get back. I won't sell it till I know what he's going to use it for."

Tony winced. "OK, Dad."

"Oh, and put the curse box in the safe for now," his dad added. "If that man has nasty plans for it, he might not want to wait. We can't risk it getting stolen."

"No, we can't," Tony said. He felt sick, but he was in too deep now and it was too late to take the lie back. "OK, I will," he said. "Bye, Dad. I'll see you when you get home."

Jazz shook her head at Tony as he put the phone down. "You're just making it worse," she said. "He'll find out the truth when he gets back."

"Not if I get the box back first," Tony said. "Then Dad will never know it was gone." It was the only way out that Tony could see.

Jazz rolled her eyes. "Oh, and how are you going to do that? We don't even know for sure that creepy bloke took it. Why doesn't your dad have cameras in this shop?"

"They don't work very well around magic." Tony said. Then he started to smile. "But you know what we do have?" He turned to point at a row of mirrors on the side wall. "Magic mirrors!"

Tony pulled Jazz over to the mirror at the end of the row. "Look, you can see the glass case in this mirror," he said. "We just need to make it show the shop a few minutes in the past."

"Do you know how to do that?" Jazz asked him.

"I think so," said Tony. He put his hand on the mirror and started to say a spell.

"Mirror made of magic glass,
Watch the people as they pass.
See where they go, see where they've been.
And show us now what you have seen!"

Tony stepped back. The Tony in the mirror didn't. His lips moved as if he was talking. Then he walked backwards across the room.

It was like watching a DVD on rewind. The mirror was showing time running backwards!

Tony saw himself and Jazz move in and out of the frame. Then it all went still for a bit. Then at last the shop door opened and closed, but no one seemed to go in or out. After that the ivory box was back in the case, and the broken glass was jumping back into place in front of it.

"That was the glass smashing in reverse," Tony said. "But there was no one there to smash it."

"I don't get it," Jazz said. "The thief was invisible?"

"I don't think so," Tony said slowly. "Where was the creepy guy?"

"Oh, yeah," said Jazz. "We should have seen him in the mirror."

"I think he doesn't show up in mirrors." Tony said.

"What does that mean?"

Tony took a deep breath. "It means that we just got robbed by a vampire."

Chapter 4
Garlic Breath

"Why would a vampire rob our shop?" Jazz asked.

Tony shook his head. "I don't know."

Vampires didn't tend to use magic much. They didn't need to. They were strong, fast, and hard to kill. Why would one of them need a magic snake?

Tony didn't know the answer to that question. But he knew where to find out. There were two sets of vampires in town – the

Red Suns and the Black Fangs. The thief had to be from one of those gangs.

"Tony, I've got to get home," Jazz said. "Will you be OK here on your own?"

"Yeah, go on," Tony said. "I think I'll close up for the night."

Jazz gave him a sharp look. "Are you going to do something stupid?"

Tony held up his hands. "All I'm planning to do right now is eat some dinner."

Jazz didn't look convinced, but she put on her coat. "OK," she said. "Make sure you don't do anything daft. See you later, Tony."

Tony waved to her as she left, then he picked up his phone and called the Hot Wok.

"Hi," he said. "I'd like to order garlic chicken. And some garlic rice. Oh, and do you still do those garlic mushrooms? Yeah, I'll have some of those too."

After he'd eaten his garlic dinner, Tony walked over to Ash Road, a long street full of pubs and clubs. Most of them were busy at this time of night. He could hear music as he passed the doors.

He walked past all the lit up clubs and went down a back alley. At the far end was a door. It had no name on it – just the shape of a sun, painted in red.

This was the home of the Red Sun vampires.

Tony took a deep breath and knocked on the door.

The door was opened by a woman. She was wearing a leather coat and had short red hair. She looked young, but there was no way to tell for sure. She could have been hundreds of years old.

Tony knew right away she was a vampire. Her eyes had a dark red glow to them, and he could see her fangs when she smiled.

It wasn't a nice smile.

"What do you want, Mr Kim?" the vampire asked. Tony had no idea how she knew his name, but he did his best to look like it didn't worry him. It was a bad idea to look weak in front of vampires.

"I'm here to see Malik," he said. Malik was the boss of the Red Sun vampires. Tony's dad had met with him a few times. But then, Tony's dad was much better at spells than Tony was – even vampires wouldn't want to mess with him. Tony might not be so lucky.

"This is no place for your kind, boy," the vampire woman sneered. But she stepped back to let Tony follow her into the hall.

It was dim inside the Red Sun base. The only light came from a few red candles, which gave off an odd, spicy smell. The smell didn't quite cover up the stink of dust and dirt.

There was a row of coffins in the first room they came to. Tony counted five of them. That was more vampires than he could fight.

In fact, one vampire was more than he could fight.

The rest of the gang was in a room at the end of the hall. Most of them jumped up as Tony came in, but one stayed in his seat.

Malik.

The head vampire was the kind of man you might see in a nightclub. He had short hair and a neat black beard. He looked young. But he wasn't.

His dark eyes had no red in them at all. His fangs didn't even show.

Old vampires could play tricks on your mind. They were good at looking human.

The others weren't as good at it. They had faces like wild animals. They stared at Tony like he was lunch.

He could swear he heard one of them growl.

"Ah, Nancy," Malik said, with a smile at the woman who'd come in with Tony. "What's this? Did you bring me a snack?"

A few of the vampires gave nasty grins. Tony stood his ground. "You wouldn't like the taste of me," he said.

Malik sniffed the air. "No, quite true," he said, with a sad frown. "You know, it's funny. I used to love garlic when I was alive. But now it just makes the blood taste bad. It's a shame."

Was Tony meant to feel sorry for him? "My heart bleeds for you," he said.

"It does?" Malik smiled and stood up. "What a lovely thing to say." He put his arm round Tony's shoulders. "Well, if you're not here for dinner, what can we do for you?"

Malik's grip was as strong as steel. His skin felt as cold and dead as a slab of meat. Tony tried not to freak out. This was crazy. Why had he come here? Malik could snap his neck like a twig if he said the wrong thing.

He knew he would have to pick his next words with great care.

So it was bad news that his mind had just gone completely blank.

Chapter 5
Snake Attack!

"Come on, don't be shy," Malik said. His eyes were fixed on Tony's and he was smiling. "Just relax ..."

Tony felt his panic drain away. Why had he been so worried? Everything was fine. He didn't have a care in the world. He just had to do what he was told ...

Wait. What? That idea hadn't come from Tony's brain! A jolt of fear woke him from his daze and he tore his eyes away from Malik's gaze. As he looked down at the floor, his mind began to clear and he could think for himself again.

Tony's heart was racing. He'd woken up just in time. A few seconds more, and Malik could have made him his slave.

He had to get out of here.

"Um, I'm here from the magic shop in town," Tony said, the words spilling out in a rush in his desire to get out. "There was a vampire in our shop tonight. I came to ask if he was one of your gang, but I don't see him here, so I'll just go ..."

He turned to leave, but Malik was too fast for him. He stepped in front of Tony and took hold of his arm.

"Now, now," Malik said, with a shake of his head. "There's no need to run off. You say a vampire came to your magic shop? Tell us more." He dug his fingers into Tony's arm, hard. "What did he want?"

Malik's voice had the same magic as his eyes. It was hard not to do what he said. "Um, he stole a magic box," Tony told him.

Nancy let out a hiss. “It’s the Black Fangs,” she said. “I told you we couldn’t trust them. They plan to use magic on us! We should have killed them all years ago.”

“Perhaps,” Malik said. He kept his eyes on Tony. “What does this magic box do?”

Tony looked up at him. “It calls up – ” Wait – what was he doing? It wasn’t safe to look at Malik! He dropped his gaze back to the floor.

As he did, he saw a silver glow on the far side of the room.

It was the head of a snake, sticking out of the wall.

Tony pointed at it. “That!” he yelped. He tried to jump back, but Malik’s grip on his arm was too strong.

The snake made no sound as it slid into the room. It was like a ghost made up of silver lines. It must have been three metres long.

Malik went still as he saw it. Tony risked looking up at his face.

Malik didn't look human now. His eyes were blood red and his fangs were bared. "Kill the snake!" he hissed at his vampires.

One of them made a grab for the snake, but it was as if there was nothing there. His hand closed on empty air.

The snake didn't have the same problem. It hissed and sank its fangs into the vampire's leg. He let out a yell.

The yell was more of shock than pain. Vampires were already dead. Snake venom shouldn't hurt one. But the vampire's eyes went wide. His skin turned grey, and then, in an instant, his body crumbled into dust. His clothes fell down to land in a heap on the floor.

The other vampires jumped back in shock. Nancy let out a snarl. "The Black Fangs mean to murder us all! Master, we have to get out of here." She tried to pull Malik away from the snake.

The other vampires turned and ran, but Malik didn't move. He still had a grip on Tony's arm.

"This magic is from your shop, boy," he said. "Send the snake away, or I'll feed you to it." He pushed Tony out in front of him.

Tony gulped. The spell had come from his shop, but that didn't mean he knew how to stop it. But he knew Malik wouldn't listen if he told him that. He had to think of a spell, and fast. The snake was less than a metre away Tony would only get one try at this.

Which spell should he use?

He knew a spell to send a ghost back to its grave.

But was the snake a real ghost?

And did a box of ashes count as a grave?

It might not be right, but it was the only thing Tony could think of. He shut his eyes and chanted the spell.

"Ghost, your bones are in the ground,
Buried long and deep.
You should be where they are found,
Go back there and sleep!"

Tony held his breath. He was too scared to open his eyes. What if the spell hadn't worked? The snake's fangs would sink in any second now ...

Or now ... Or ... now?

Tony opened his eyes. The snake was gone.

"Wow," he said. He blinked a few times. "I can't believe that worked."

Malik let go of his arm. "Not bad, wizard," he said, with a thin smile. "I may let you live after all."

Chapter 6
The Black Fangs

Tony couldn't leave right away, much as he wanted to – his way out was blocked. The Red Sun vampires were angry, shouting and yelling as they tried to decide what to do next. Tony didn't want them to notice him if he could help it, so he sat in the corner and kept his mouth shut.

"The Black Fangs must be made to pay!" Nancy shouted. "We should go to their nest and rip them to shreds."

"Perhaps we will," said Malik. His voice was calm. "But first we must be sure that this is their work. We've been at peace for more than 70 years. I won't break the truce without proof."

Nancy let out a hiss. "Who else would dare attack us like this?"

"I don't know," said Malik. "But I plan to find out. Wizard!" He spun round to face Tony.

Tony jumped. "Me?"

Malik gave him a cool look. "It seems we share a common goal," he said. "You wish to know who stole your magic box, and now so do I. Unlike us, you can go out when the sun is up. You must find the thief by dark tomorrow."

Tony gulped. "And if I don't?"

Malik gave a thin smile. "Then I will have to assume that the Black Fangs are to blame. We will go to war – and I don't think you want that."

That was true. If the two gangs went to war, both sides would need more troops. They would kill lots of people to make new vampires, and take humans as slaves to fight for them.

Who knew how many people could die?

Tony gave a sick smile. "Right," he said. "So, no pressure then."

It was hard for Tony to sleep when he got back home, but he went to bed anyway – he knew he needed the rest. Plus he couldn't drop in on the Black Fangs when it was still dark – they would still be awake. And two gangs of vampires was more than he could take in one night.

He hoped the Black Fangs weren't to blame, but who else could it be? Was there a new vampire gang in town? That could be even worse news.

It was after four o'clock when at last Tony fell asleep. His dreams were full of blood and slime and snakes. When he woke up the next morning, he didn't feel rested at all, but he knew he had to get moving. He rang the shop as soon as he was dressed.

"Jazz, hi," he said when she picked up the phone. "Um, look. Some stuff came up, and ..."

"Let me guess. You're taking the day off," she said. She sounded annoyed.

"I'm not taking it off," Tony said. "I'm just, er … not going to be at work."

"Oh, well. That's different, then," Jazz said.

"You're rolling your eyes, aren't you?" Tony asked.

"You're not here, so you won't ever know," Jazz said. "I suppose you want me to deal with the slime?"

"Oh. Yeah. I forgot about that. If you could, that would be great."

"I want a pay rise," Jazz said, and hung up.

"Yeah. Me too," Tony said to himself.

He left the house and went to get on his motorbike.

The Black Fangs had their nest on the north side of town, in an old empty house. The windows were boarded up to block out the sun.

The front door wasn't locked. The Black Fangs didn't need to be scared of people breaking in. It was the people who broke in who should be scared of them.

But Tony had no choice.

The door creaked as he pushed it open, and he froze. Vampires slept during the day, but that didn't mean they couldn't wake up.

He waited, but he didn't hear a sound. Of course, that didn't mean much. Vampires could move with no noise if they wanted to.

He took a deep breath and walked in.

Inside the house it was dark. Tony couldn't see a thing once he shut the door. He held his hand out and said a simple spell.

"Dark of night, light of day.
Give me light to show the way!"

A ball of blue light floated up from his hand. It wasn't very bright, but that was a good thing. He didn't want to wake anyone up if he could help it.

The house was a mess. It looked like there had been a fight – or a party. There was a faint smell of blood that made him feel sick.

There were no coffins on the ground floor – they must be up in the bedrooms. If the Black

Fangs had the curse box, it was sure to be up there too.

Tony started to climb the stairs. They creaked with every step, and by the time he got to the top, his chest was tight with nerves. But it looked like he was still safe. As he peered into the first room, he saw a closed coffin. The vampires hadn't woken up.

Yet.

There was a big wardrobe at the back of the room. Tony headed for it. Maybe he'd get lucky and find the box in the first place he looked.

He watched the wardrobe door carefully as he pulled it open. He didn't want it to bump the coffin.

That was why he didn't see what was in the wardrobe.

Not till a hand shot out of it and grabbed him by the throat.

Chapter 7
Out of Ideas

Tony couldn't yell out in shock – he didn't have the breath to do it. The hand round his neck was cutting off all his air.

It was a woman's hand. She had long black hair and skin so white she looked dead. She was wearing a necklace made of black stones, and her eyes were red as blood.

Tony knew who she must be. This was Sophie, leader of the Black Fangs.

And he was in big trouble.

"So, you came back," Sophie said. Her voice was an angry snarl. "That will be the last mistake you make, human."

What did she mean, 'came back'? Tony had never been here before! He tried to say so, but all he could do was wheeze.

"Did you think you would find us all dead?" Sophie asked. "Your magic snake was weak and slow. It killed only the human that we planned to eat." She gave him a sharp smile. "How nice of you to come here, so we can feed on you instead."

Oh, hell. The snake had been sent after the Black Fangs too? Then they couldn't be the ones who had set it on the Red Suns! So who was behind the attacks? And how could Tony convince Sophie that it wasn't him?

All of a sudden, Sophie let go of Tony's neck. He fell to his knees, gasping for air.

"Well, human," Sophie said in a cold voice. "Any last words?"

"It wasn't me!"

Tony sounded like he was about four years old, but it did make Sophie stop and give him a sharp look.

"Really?" she said. "That's the best defence you have?"

"It's true!" Tony told her. His voice came out as a rasp and it was still hard to catch his breath. "I'm from the magic shop. The snake was stolen from us. By a vampire."

"The Red Suns," she said. "I should have known."

"No!" Tony yelled. "Um, I mean, it wasn't them. I've just seen them – the snake went after their base too. I think someone is trying to start a war."

Sophie glared at him. "And how do I know this is not a Red Sun trick?" she asked.

"Um ... because it's not?"

Sophie stared at him for a few seconds, then rolled her eyes.

"You sound so stupid, I think I believe you. If this was a trick, you would know what to say." She folded her arms. "So who is behind this plan to make us fight the Red Suns?"

"Er ... I don't know," Tony said. "But I can find out! If you'll just let me go ..."

"Find out who is behind this, and bring me their name before dark," Sophie ordered. "Or I will declare war on the Red Suns – and on you." Her eyes blazed red.

Great. Now Tony had to report back to two vampires.

And he had no idea what to do next.

In the end, Tony went back to the magic shop. He needed to work out a way to find the thief, and fast. But if it wasn't one of the Red Suns or the Black Fangs, who else could it be?

The shop was silent when he walked in. There was no sign of Jazz. "Hello?" he shouted. "Anyone there?"

"I'm in here!" Jazz said, stepping out from the back room. She had pink rubber gloves on and there was slime on her top.

Tony smirked. "Trying out a new look?"

Jazz glared at him. "I am trying to clean up that mess in the back room. What did you put in that spell? The slime is like glue."

Tony held up his hands. "I didn't mean it!" he said. And then idea hit him. "In fact, maybe I didn't even do it – I bet the thief put something in it! He must have hoped the spell would go wrong and we'd run to check on it."

"Well, his plan worked," Jazz said.

"Yeah." Tony shook his head. "It's a pity we don't know what he put in it."

"Flare powder," Jazz said.

Tony stared at her. "How do you know that?"

Jazz rolled her eyes. "We just got robbed, Tony. I've spent all day checking our stock. That's the only other thing missing."

Flare powder. It was used to make flames burn brighter, but Tony didn't like to use it. He always seemed to get it all over him.

He started to smile.

"Jazz. Do we have any flare powder left?"

"Um, yeah. There's another pot." Jazz walked over to the shelves and lifted it down for him. "Why?"

Tony tried to get the lid off the pot. "Wait and see ..." The lid came off with a pop and red powder went all over his hands and shirt. "It always does this when you open it," he told her.

"Great, Tony," Jazz said. "Make more mess, why don't you?"

Tony just grinned. "The thief must have opened one of these pots," he said. "And if he did, I bet he got some on him. There can't be a lot of flare powder in this town. We can use magic to track it down. Find the flare powder – find the thief!"

Chapter 8
The Thief's Den

Tony got out his dad's map of the town. It had spells cast on it so it could be used for magic. He held the pot of flare powder over it as he spoke.

"This map shows us the world outside.
We use it now to be our guide.
Seek out magic of your own kind,
And show us what we seek to find!"

Tony tipped the powder out of the pot. It fell down over the map like red snow, making patterns where it landed.

A thick line of powder started at the shop, leading out of the door and down the alley. From there it went to a street called Pine Row. Then a thinner line went on to the Red Sun base, where it stopped.

"What does that mean?" Jazz asked.

Tony looked at the map with a frown. "I guess the thief went to Pine Row first," he said. "He must have got rid of most of the powder there, but there was still a bit left on him when he went to the Red Sun base."

It seemed a bit odd that he would go to the base at all. Why would he need to? He could send the snake from as far away as he liked.

He must have wanted to see if it worked. Tony pulled a face. The thief must have been right outside when the snake appeared! If only they'd gone out to look. But Nancy had started that fight with Malik – she'd wanted to go to war with the Black Fangs right away.

If Tony didn't find the thief, she'd get her wish.

There were less than four hours left till dark.

"All right," Tony said to Jazz. "I'm going to Pine Row. If we're lucky, I'll find the thief there."

"What if we're not lucky?" Jazz asked.

Tony tried not to think about it. "Let's just hope we're lucky," he said.

Tony took his motorbike to Pine Row. It wasn't far, but there was no time to lose. If he didn't find the thief here, he was done for.

And what if he did find the thief? This was a vampire that had killed its own kind. Malik and Sophie might have listened to Tony, but this one would just rip his head off.

He'd better not wake it up when he found its nest. If he found its nest.

There were no shops or houses on Pine Row, just office blocks. The one at the end was closed up. Big letters in the window said 'Space for Rent'.

That looked like a good place to start.

Tony made his way into the office block. There was a fence with a locked gate, but it was made of wire mesh, so it was easy to climb over.

It would be twice as easy for a vampire.

There was a broken window round the back of the block which Tony climbed through – but it let the sun in too. A vampire wouldn't make a nest where the sun could get to it.

So where would it go?

Underground, if it could. Tony looked round.

Yes, he was right. There was a set of stairs leading down to a basement.

It was dark down at the bottom of the stairs. Tony said the same light spell he had used back at the Black Fang nest. Then he stood at the top and waited.

He didn't hear anything move.

After a minute, Tony made his way down the stairs, one slow step at a time. When he got to the bottom, he swore. There was no coffin down here, no place for a vampire to sleep. This couldn't be its nest.

But then he saw a heap of cloth on the floor. It was the long coat the thief had been wearing!

Tony went to pick the coat up, and as he did, he heard a click. He looked down.

The ivory curse box was sitting on the floor. The click had been the lid falling open. The coat must have been tucked in so it would open the box when he pulled it.

The thief had left it as a trap.

Tony turned and ran for the stairs, but he knew he didn't have time to get out. The silver shape of the snake was already forming. He'd seen how fast it could move – there was no way he'd make it all the way up the stairs.

Halfway up the stairs, Tony stopped and turned back. He shouted the same spell he'd used before.

"Ghost, your bones are in the ground,

Buried long and deep.

You should be where they are found,

Go back there and sleep!"

It had got rid of the snake in seconds last time. So it should vanish just about … now.

It didn't. It swung round to look at him and hissed. Then it started to move towards him.

"Oh, hell."

Chapter 9
Death Trap

The snake was already at the foot of the stairs. Tony knew he didn't have time to get to the top, and he couldn't run back down with the snake on its way up.

There was only one way left to go.

Tony looked to his side. There was a rail that ran down the side of the stairs to stop people falling.

But it couldn't stop people who jumped.

He dived off the side of the stairs.

There was no time to try and land with care. He hit the ground hard, and his ankle made a horrible crunch. He yelled out in pain and crumpled to the ground.

From where he was lying, he could see the open curse box. If he could close it, that might get rid of the snake. But it was out of his reach where he was – he would have to crawl forward. And his ankle felt like it was on fire.

Tony gave a push with his good leg, dragging the bad one along the ground. There was a burst of hot pain, and dark spots danced in front of his eyes.

He couldn't pass out now! He took a few deep breaths and his head cleared. He reached out to try and grab the box.

It was still just a fraction too far away. Tony could see the snake getting closer. He was almost out of time.

One last chance.

Tony stretched out as far as his arm would reach. The tips of his fingers just touched the side of the box, but there was no way he could get a grip to pull it closer to him.

As the snake opened its mouth wide, he pushed the box instead. It rocked away from him ... and fell shut.

The snake vanished just as it was about to bite down on his arm. Tony could swear he felt its fangs brush his skin.

He rolled over onto his back and closed his eyes. “That was too close, Tony,” he said. “Way too close.”

He lay there for a few seconds while he got his breath back. Then it was time to sit up and see what he’d done to his ankle. He went to pull the leg of his jeans up to have a look.

His right hand didn’t seem to want to work.

In fact, the whole of his right arm felt a bit funny. Sort of cold and numb ...

Tony pulled his sleeve back to look at his arm. There was a dot of blood on the skin. One of the snake’s fangs must have got him after all.

“Oh, that is so not fair,” he said.

This time he did pass out.

Tony woke up when a foot poked him in the chest. He opened his eyes to see Sophie standing over him.

She gave a smile that showed off her fangs.

"How odd," she said. "I could swear I gave you a job to do, yet here you are, fast asleep."

The room seemed to wobble as Tony sat up. He felt dizzy and weak, but at least he was alive. Why hadn't the snake's venom killed him?

He looked down at his arm. The snake's fang had only just broken the skin. He must have only got a small dose of the venom.

He had been lucky But he would have to talk fast if he wanted to stay alive. Sophie looked very, very angry.

"I wasn't asleep!" Tony said. "I was hurt ... Look, I found the thief's base! This is the stuff he was wearing at the shop."

He pointed at the coat. Then he saw the thief's hat there too. And the big grey beard.

Huh. The beard was a fake? That meant the thief could have been anyone. Tony could have met him again and not even known it.

In fact, maybe he had. Things started to click into place in his head. He was getting an idea ...

But Sophie didn't give him time to think. "Old clothes!" she said with a growl. "These are no use to me. I asked you to find the thief – and you have failed." Her eyes went red.

"Wait!" said Tony, alarmed. "You said I could have until – "

But then it hit him. Sophie had come to find him. She couldn't do that if the sun was still up, so ...

"It's after dark already?" he asked, feeling sick.

"Yes, it is," Sophie said. "And you've made me waste my time sniffing you out. Just for that, I plan to kill you. Slowly and painfully."

But then there was a creak from the top of the stairs. They both turned to look.

It was Malik.

"Now, now, Sophie," Malik said. "I'm afraid I can't let you kill him. He did come to see me first." He gave Tony a cold smile. "That means I get to kill him."

Tony held his breath as Malik walked down the steps. These were the leaders of the two rival gangs – the two oldest vampires in town. Were they going to fight over him?

The two vampires got closer and closer, and Malik growled as he grabbed hold of Sophie ...

They started to kiss.

Tony stared. "OK, wow," he said, blinking. "Didn't see that one coming."

They broke apart and turned to look at him. Their eyes had gone blood red.

"Now you know our secret," Malik said

"One more reason for us to kill you," Sophie said with a smile.

"Wait!" Tony said. There was one thing that might save his life. "I think I know who the thief is!"

He just hoped he was right.

Chapter 10
Love and War

"You're lying," Sophie hissed.

"No!" Tony said. "I just worked it out." He pointed at the fake beard. "The thief had a fake beard, so I never knew who I was looking for. It could have been anyone! Even one of the vampires that I met last night."

Malik's eyes narrowed. "Go on."

"When I was at your base, I got rid of the snake with a spell, right?" said Tony.

Malik gave a small nod.

"Wrong," Tony said. "That wasn't me. I tried that spell again, and it didn't work. I think the thief closed the box at the same time as I said the spell, to make it look like it was me. But to time it that well – "

"The thief must have been in the room with you," said Sophie.

Malik growled. "If you're trying to blame me ..."

Tony shook his head. "Not you." That wouldn't make sense – Malik was the boss. If he wanted to start a war, he could just say so.

But Malik hadn't been the only one in the room. Nancy had been there too.

Nancy, who had blamed the Black Fangs right away.

Nancy, who had made a show of trying to save Malik from the snake.

Nancy, who had known Tony's name when she met him at the door.

Tony looked at Malik. "Nancy called me 'Mr Kim'," he said. "How did she know my name? You didn't know who I was, but the thief did, because I told the thief my name in the shop."

Sophie let out a roar. "Her!" She spun round to face Malik. "I told you that you trusted her too much!"

"I have my reasons," Malik said. He glared at Tony. "Where is your proof, boy?"

"Um," said Tony. He didn't have proof. It was just a guess.

He was saved by the sound of a crash from upstairs. "What was that?" he yelled, looking up.

"I told my vampires to come after me if I was gone too long," said Malik.

Sophie looked at him. "Did you?" she asked. "So did I."

Both gangs of vampires, told to come to the same place?

Tony swore.

Sophie and Malik ran up the stairs. Tony moved slower with his bad ankle. He picked up the curse box on his way.

When he got to the top of the stairs, there was a fight going on. Nancy was in the middle of it. "Kill them!" she yelled. "They broke the truce."

"You broke it first!" one of the Black Fangs yelled back.

"Stop this!" Malik ordered his gang.

"Black Fangs, back off!" Sophie screamed at hers.

The two gangs moved apart, but it was clear they didn't want to. They stood at the sides of the room and glared at each other.

Only Nancy stayed in the middle. She looked at Malik. "We should wipe them out, Master," she said. "The Black Fangs broke their word."

Sophie let out a hiss. "You are the one who broke the truce," she said. "Don't try to frame us."

Nancy laughed. "Do you really think my master will believe your lies?"

"Are they lies?" asked Malik.

Nancy spun to stare at him. "She's the enemy!" she said. "You would take her word over mine? She has no proof!"

"She doesn't," Tony said. "But I do." He held up the curse box and started to lift the lid off. "Snake!" he said. "Show us who sent you. Go to the person who's been giving you your orders!"

Nancy didn't wait for him to open the box the rest of the way. She turned and ran out of the room.

"After her!" Malik said to the nearest vampire. It was one of the Black Fangs.

The vampire scowled. "We don't take orders from you."

Sophie stepped up next to Malik. She put her arm round him and kissed his cheek. "You do now," she said. "From now on, our two clans are one. You will all take your orders from me and Malik."

Malik smiled. "Hurry, all of you! Go after Nancy. I want her dead before the sun rises."

Both sets of vampires ran out.

Malik turned back to Tony. “You’ve been a great help to us, wizard,” he said.

Sophie smiled. “In fact,” she said, “we’ll even let you live. For now.”

They left to follow the other vampires.

Tony sat down on the floor. His legs felt weak. He had the curse box back, and he was alive. But he’d also helped two vampire gangs to join forces. That didn’t seem like such a good thing.

He knew he had to tell his dad. He got his mobile out.

“Um, Dad?” he said when his father picked up. “I’ve got some bad news. You know how we used to have two vampire gangs?”

His dad laughed. “Oh, they got together at last, did they?”

“You knew about Sophie and Malik?” Tony asked, shocked.

“I had an idea,” said his dad. “Don’t worry about it, Tony. It’s not as if you’re to blame.”

"Er," Tony began. But he didn't get a chance to confess.

"By the way," his dad added. "I spoke to Boris about that curse box. He said not to worry about it getting stolen. It turns out there's a spell on it."

"There is?"

"Yes. If it's gone for more than one full day, it will pop right back to the place that it was taken from. Neat, huh?"

Tony didn't say anything.

"So!" said his dad. "Anything else you want to tell me?"

Tony looked down at the box in his hand. "Er ... no," he said. "Nothing at all."

The box vanished with a small pop.

Our books are tested
for children and young people by
children and young people.

Thanks to everyone who consulted on
a manuscript for their time and effort in
helping us to make our books better
for our readers.